Alvah and Arvilla

Mary Lyn Ray

ILLUSTRATED BY

Barry Root

Harcourt Brace & Company

SAN DIEGO   NEW YORK   LONDON

Requests for permission to make copies of any part of the work should
be mailed to: Permissions Department, Harcourt Brace & Company,
6277 Sea Harbor Drive, Orlando, Florida 32887-6777.

Library of Congress Cataloging-in-Publication Data
Ray, Mary Lyn.
Alvah and Arvilla/by Mary Lyn Ray;
illustrated by Barry Root. — 1st ed.   p. cm.
Summary: Alvah and Arvilla have never been able to see the Pacific
Ocean because of having to care for their farm animals, until they
build a *voiture* that will enable them all to travel west to see it.
ISBN 0-15-202655-X
[1. Ocean — Fiction. 2. Overland journeys to the Pacific — Fiction.
3. Farm animals — Fiction.] I. Root, Barry, ill II. Title.
PZ7.R210154A   1994   [E] — dc20   93-31874

Printed in Singapore

First edition
A B C D E

The illustrations in this book were done in watercolor and
gouache on D'Arches 140-pound hot-press watercolor paper.
The display type was set in Nuptial Script and the text type was set in
Cochin by Harcourt Brace Photocomposition Center, San Diego, California.
Color separations were made by Bright Arts, Ltd., Singapore.
Printed and bound by Tien Wah Press, Singapore
This book was printed with soya-based inks on Leykam recycled paper,
which contains more than 20 percent postconsumer waste and has
a total recycled content of at least 50 percent.
Production supervision by Warren Wallerstein and Ginger Boyer
Designed by Michael Farmer

For Donna and Phil, who married a farm

— M. L. R.

For Sarah Westbrook

— B. R.

ARVILLA was canning peaches when she got the idea.

  She filled the jars, put on the lids, and took them to the cellar, where she stored pickles and preserves for winter.

  Upstairs, she cleared the kitchen, made supper, and called Alvah.

  The idea didn't go away.

Out the window the moon rose over the pasture. A small wind moved through the grass, the way she imagined waves moved across the ocean.

Arvilla wanted to go on a trip. She wanted to see the Pacific. The last time she and Alvah had been away was the night they were married, thirty-one years before.

Once a month they went to Franklin, when the milk check came. And some years Arvilla managed a day in Boston before Christmas, to see the lights and do some shopping. But they never went on trips like their neighbors took—trips they could send postcards from.

"You can't have a farm and travel," Alvah said.
   There were cows to milk morning and night, and horses
and hens and sheep to feed.
   So for thirty-one years Arvilla and Alvah stayed home.
   And for thirty-one years Arvilla imagined the ocean.
   Until suddenly, at supper, she turned to Alvah and said, "If it's
the animals keeping us here, we'll take the animals with us."

Alvah kept eating his biscuit. He knew they couldn't do that. But Arvilla had it figured.

Once in Boston at the arboretum she saw a house built all of glass, where coconut trees and hyacinths grew inside in winter.

She drew a picture for Alvah, substituting cows—their cows—for tropical trees. Then she added wheels.

And Alvah, who usually was cautious of ideas, said, "Ayuh."

The next day he bought glass and putty and lumber, and he began to hammer. Every day he hammered.

Soon he announced, "Rig's ready."

Arvilla admired what Alvah had built. Her only disappointment was to call it a rig. She remembered something French she heard in the city, and privately she called it their *voiture*.

When she went to feed the chickens, she told them, "Your *voiture* is ready." But they seemed unimpressed.

Alvah and Arvilla began to pack.

They dismantled the bed in their bedroom, carried it out the door, and reassembled it in the glass car. Next they brought a table, two chairs, two forks, two spoons, two knives, two plates, two cups, a skillet, a kettle, a stove.

They packed clothes for cold days and clothes for warm days.

They loaded beans, pickles, maple creams, popcorn, dried
cod, and apples—a barrel of Northern Spies and another of
Roxbury Russets. They brought jars of summer from the
cellar—jams, jellies, vegetables, and fruits. Hay for the cows
and horses and sheep. Dry corn for the hens. And a box
up front of useful things: a map, a bottle of ink, a pen, and
a roll of stamps.

Then they loaded the animals.

Up the ramp came the cows—Betty, Blossom, Dear, Rose,
Fleur, Ruth, Dora, Belle, and Sweet. Then the sheep—Dahlia,
Daisy, Maud, Juno, Jacqueline, and Esther. Then the cats—
Black, Snake, Wenatchee, Mississippi, and Columbia. Then the
dogs—Roger and Herb. And then the hens who, being very
plural, were unnamed.

Last of all Alvah brought the horses—Horace and Albert—
and hitched them to pull. Arvilla climbed onto the little front
porch. Alvah took the reins. And when he called "Giddyup,"
they rolled out of the yard.

After a while they came to a wide river. Horace stopped and
looked around with a look that meant "Are we there yet?"
Arvilla shook her head "No." So they crossed the river and
continued.

Day after day Arvilla and Alvah drove west, watching the land go flat.

Along about Oklahoma (except it wasn't Oklahoma yet—it was called a territory), Albert looked around with a look that meant "Are we there yet?" And Arvilla shook her head "No." They had to cross the prairie. So they kept on.

All they saw was grass and sky, and then no grass.

In a dry, dry place—not yet a state, not yet Arizona—Maud came forward and looked a look that meant "Are we there yet?" And Arvilla shook her head "No." They had to cross the desert.

So day after day they drove across sand, until suddenly they saw mountains. Roger wagged his tail with a wag that meant "Are we there yet?" Arvilla shook her head "No." They had to cross the mountains.

So up, up, up they went. And down, down, down.

Then Arvilla saw it.

The land came to a wet, sudden end. Waves. Sand. Palms that looked like pineapples. Ocean! The Pacific Ocean.

As soon as the horses stopped, they all got out and looked. And when they recovered from shyness, they waded into the water.

"Ayuh," said Alvah.

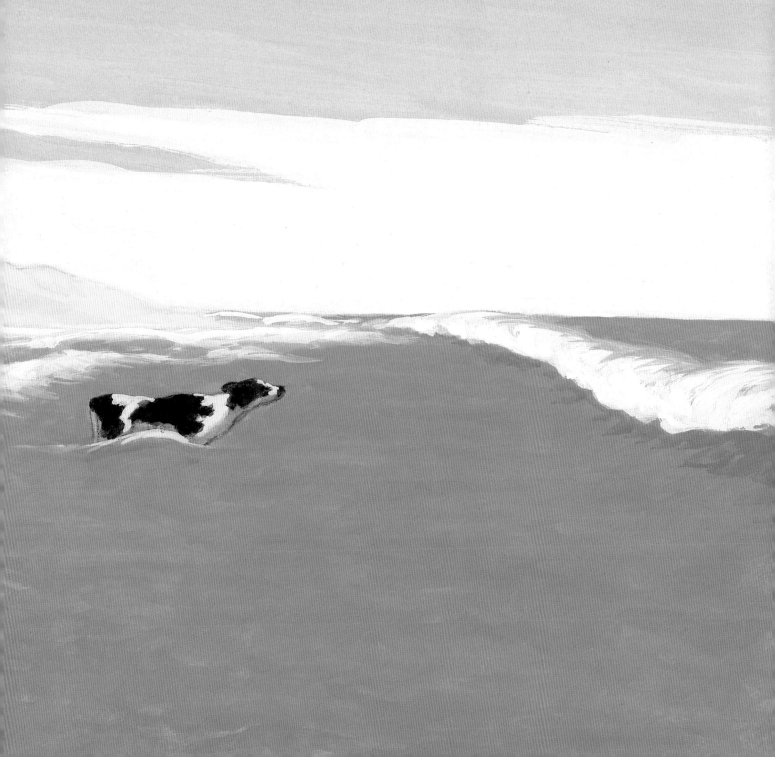

That night they ate avocados and oranges.

And the next day, observing local custom, they all lay on the beach while Arvilla wrote postcards.

Days came and went like lazy tides. But after a while the cows began to fidget. The sheep began to fidget. Alvah began to fidget. And Arvilla had used up her stamps.

They'd seen what they came to see. It was time for Betty, Blossom, Dear, Rose, Fleur, Ruth, Dora, Belle, Sweet, Dahlia, Daisy, Maud, Juno, Jacqueline, Esther, Black, Snake, Wenatchee, Mississippi, Columbia, Roger, Herb, Horace, Albert, Alvah, Arvilla, and the flutter of hens to go home.

Back up the mountains and down, back over the desert and prairie, back across rivers little and big.

Day after day they drove east, until they saw their hills return.

And on the last hill, their farm.

Alvah unhitched the horses. Arvilla led the cows and sheep to pasture. The chickens scuttled everywhere. The cats went to

examine the barn, and the dogs nosed the yard.

Arvilla and Alvah unpacked. They took their bed back to their bedroom and put the table and chairs in the kitchen. They returned the cups, the plates, the silver, the kettle, the skillet, the stove. They hung their clothes in their closets. But no food was left—only empty jars to store in the cellar.

It was time to begin the garden.

The next day Alvah parked the glass car in the bright spring
sun and removed the wheels. Then he covered half the floor
with flats for seedlings and planted a start on summer —
tomatoes, lettuce, squash.
    The other half he offered to Arvilla, to set her geraniums in.

But Arvilla had another idea.
She opened the apple barrels they ate empty going west.
She had filled them with sand from the Pacific, which she
swept across the floor to make a little beach.

And here she and Alvah and sometimes a cow or a cat or a
dog lie and remember the ocean.
    "Ayuh," says Alvah. "Ayuh."